Antoinette Portis

Wait

A NEAL PORTER BOOK
ROARING BROOK PRESS
NEW YORK

For my mom, who waited

Copyright © 2015 by Antoinette Portis
A Neal Porter Book
Published by Roaring Brook Press
Roaring Brook Press is a division of Holtzbrinck Publishing Holdings
Limited Partnership, 120 Broadway, New York, NY 10271
The art for this book was created with pencil, charcoal, and ink.
Color was added digitally.
mackids.com   All rights reserved

Library of Congress Cataloging-in-Publication Data
Portis, Antoinette.
    Wait / by Antoinette Portis. — First edition.
        pages cm
    "A Neal Porter Book."
Summary: "A simple, sweet picture book about the joys of waiting and
taking in what is around you"— Provided by publisher.
    ISBN 978-1-59643-921-4 (hardback)
[1. Patience—Fiction. 2. Attention—Fiction.] I. Title.
PZ7.P8362Wai 2015
    [E]–dc23
                    2014027119

Roaring Brook Press books may be purchased for business or
promotional use. For information on bulk purchases please
contact Macmillan Corporate and Premium Sales
Department at (800) 221-7945 x5442 or by email
at specialmarkets@macmillan.com.

First edition 2015
Book design by Antoinette Portis and Jennifer Browne
Printed in China by Toppan Leefung Printing Ltd.,
Dongguan City, Guangdong Province

10 9 8 7 6

Hurry!

Wait.

Hurry!

Wait.

Hurry!

Wait.

Wait.

Hurry!

Wait.

Hurry!

Hurry!

Wait.

Yes.
Wait.